The War of the Wizards

The War of
the Wizards

BY CAROL GASKIN

Illustrations by T. Alexander Price

TROLL ASSOCIATES

Library of Congress Cataloging in Publication Data

Gaskin, Carol.
   The war of the wizards.

   (The Forgotten forest)
   Summary: The reader, as apprentice to the wizard
Caladrius, becomes involved in a war of the wizards,
during the course of which the reader's choices determine
the development of the plot.
   1. Plot-your-own stories.   2. Children's stories,
American.   [1. Plot-your-own stories.   2. Magic—Fiction.
3. Fantasy]   I. Price, T. Alexander, ill.   II. Title.
III. Series.
PZ7.G213War   1985   [Fic]   84-2663
ISBN 0-8167-0318-3 (lib. bdg.)
ISBN 0-8167-0319-1 (pbk.)

10   9   8   7   6   5   4   3   2   1

Welcome to the Forgotten Forest

In this adventure, your name is Simon. You are an apprentice to the great wizard Caladrius.

As you read, you will be asked to make important decisions: Do you want to use the transformation spell? Or the mirror amulet? Would you prefer to go seek the Wizard of Earth? Or the Wizardess of Night?

There are many paths you can follow in the Forgotten Forest. You may end up lost in a dismal swamp —or you may be a hero. The choice is *yours*.

When the adventure ends, you can always return to the beginning and follow a new path. Choose well, and the best of luck in your journey!

"Simon! Why don't you answer me?"

The wizard Caladrius is calling you from the herb garden. You are in his workshed, frantically searching for a broom to sweep up the broken bottle of dried toad dust you have accidentally dropped on the floor.

You are the wizard's apprentice, and your morning task is to gather wart root from his garden. But this morning the workshed door was open a crack. You know you are not supposed to snoop in Caladrius' shed when he is not there. But you've always been fascinated by the rows of bottles, jars, tins, and canisters, each neatly labeled, lining the worktables and shelves. You were curiously examining this array of magical ingredients, imagining the fine spells you could weave, when, *"S-I-I-MON!"*—Caladrius' sandpaper voice rasped into your daydream. *Crash!* The bottle of toad powder seemed to leap from your hand all by itself. The wizard will have you grinding toad skins for a week if he finds out.

You've never thought of Caladrius as an impressive-looking wizard. Behind his back you fondly call him "Rattles," because his ancient joints and brittle bones clatter and creak when he moves. But he is one of the best wizards in the forest, and his fame as a teacher has spread all the way to the seas. You've learned lots of wizardry in your seven-year apprenticeship.

A-clackity-ackity-rickety-rackety—the wizard's approach sounds like someone shaking a bag of marbles. The door to the shed slams open, and a gust of wind scatters the spilled toad powder all over your left boot and across the floor. Now you're in for it.

Caladrius' slight figure seems to fill the doorway. He is so angry he's shaking. His bones rattle and his teeth chatter even though he is standing still. His starched gown sticks out at crazy angles, and sparks fly from his cobweb whiskers.

In one thin hand he holds his crystal ball. Maybe he looked into the crystal and saw you snooping in the shed? But he doesn't start to scold you, or drag you by the ear back out to the garden. He doesn't even seem to notice the dusty mess.

"Fools!" he croaks. "I was afraid it would come to this." He fastens his pale, grave eyes on yours. Then he speaks quietly. "Simon. War has begun."

You stare at him, startled. A war? Here? How can that be? "Wh-what war?" you stammer.

"A war among the wizards," he says. "Look, look into the crystal ball and I will show you."

You look, but all you see is a swirling, purple cloud.

"There once was a time when wizards were few and far between," Caladrius begins. "But our land attracts all things magical, and our numbers have increased. We each have our specialties, so there has always been room—indeed, welcome—for another. That is why, in our small land alone, we can boast of *six* wizards. And you, Simon, if we are not all doomed, will make the seventh." Caladrius looks gloomily into the crystal ball. He begins to count wizards on his long, bony fingers. His knuckles crackle like tumbling dice.

"First, there is myself, the Wizard of Changes." As you gaze, Caladrius' familiar form appears in the crystal. "My specialties are transformations, sudden reversals, tricks of motion and time. I can change a man into a lizard, or hours into minutes.

"Then there is Lunay, my former apprentice." A beautiful maiden with silvery hair shimmers in the ball. "She is only two centuries older than you, Simon, and very gifted. She became a Wizardess of Night. She invents nocturnal spells and tends the creatures of darkness.

"The other four are Wizards of Elements. Hod, a Wizard of Earth, uses solid matter to create his magic. He is a famed herbalist, and can model living creatures out of clay. And Rilla, a Wizardess of Water, has talent with all liquid things."

The image in the crystal of Hod, a squat, muscular man, is splashed over by Rilla, a shimmering woman in a foamy dress. Next you see the graceful form of another man, with hair of gray feathers.

"That is Syrrus, a Wizard of Air," Caladrius continues. "He concentrates on airy things—winds, birds, gases, cyclones. And, last, there is Fray, a Wizard of Fire. He has great power with heat, metals, dragons, volcanoes, and the like." A ruddy, muscular figure flickers in the glass. His red mustache and beard lick out from his face like flames.

Caladrius sighs. "Gradually, competition and conflict have arisen. Lunay complains that Syrrus steals her bats. Hod claims that Rilla's rainstorms are drenching his clay pit. Rilla responds that she is only creating relief from Fray's merciless sunshine."

Next you see a confused, unhappy farmer in the crystal ball. The crops on one side of his field are drowned, and on the other side they are scorched.

"Now one wizard wishes to become all-powerful, and that one is hot-tempered Fray. He thinks the best way to settle these differences is for him to reign supreme. In order to prove his supremacy, Fray wants to battle with each of us, one at a time. And today he has attacked Syrrus. Now Hod, claiming that *he* is the greatest, readies an army of clay men to send against Rilla. Soon we will all be at war."

You look into the crystal again. You see Hod, the Wizard of Earth, at a potter's wheel, murmuring incantations as he shapes a rude being of clay. Then the crystal ball glows bright orange. You see a blazing fireball hurtle through the sky from Fray's brimstone fortress toward Syrrus' Palace of Clouds. Syrrus whips up a whirlwind that sends the fireball roaring to earth like a comet. The neighboring forest folk—gnomes, woodcutters, and animals—tremble in terror.

"For the peace of the forest, this must be stopped!" cries Caladrius. "And, Simon, you must choose what *you* will do. I am old, and cannot travel far. I plan to remain and defend my castle against Fray. You may be in danger if you stay here, and I will be fine by myself. I will provide you with spells to help you through these dark days."

Caladrius turns to leave, then pauses at the doorway. "And while you're deciding, clean up that toad dust."

Go to page 7.

You are worried as you bend to your sweeping. You also can't help noticing that the part of your boot the toad dust landed on has disappeared. You turn your attention to the choice you must make. Perhaps Caladrius really does need your help. But someone must try to prevent Hod and Rilla from beginning a battle with each other. And Fray must be stopped before he can do more damage.

If you decide to stay with Caladrius and join in the defense of his castle, turn to page 63.

If you want to accept Caladrius' spells and then try to talk reason to Hod and Rilla, turn to page 10.

If you want to use the toad dust to become invisible, and set out to stop Fray, turn to page 22.

8

"I'm very sorry," you say to the swamp monkey. "I thought your tail was a vine." Pirate squawks in agreement.

The creature stops chattering and answers, "Good mistake. Tail camouflaged. Need vine?"

Now he seems polite, no longer the angry wild beast who has had his tail pulled. "Yes, please," you say.

He loosens a nearby vine and tosses it to you. You tie the end around your waist and swing across to the swamp monkey's tree, landing as awkwardly as before.

"Cheecheecheecheechee!" the monkey screeches. You reach for your spells, ready for an attack, until you realize that he is just laughing at your jungle technique.

"Swing bad," he explains. "Must relax. Watch me."

First the swamp monkey imitates you, with funny, exaggerated movements. He ties a vine to his waist, springs far from the tree, and lands on a nearby branch on his hindquarters.

You giggle at his antics but watch his return trip closely. It is smooth and effortless. He lands next to you, on his feet.

You practice together until you have improved. Then you collapse on a thick tree limb, out of breath.

"See? Easy," says the monkey. "I Abbez. You who? Go where?"

"I am Simon the Apprentice," you say, out of breath, "and I seek the Fortress of Fray. Do you know where it is, Abbez?"

He looks worried. "I know. Fire place. No go. Fray bad."

"I must," you tell him, "for he may destroy the Forgotten Forest if I cannot stop him." Abbez reluctantly agrees to guide you through the swamp.

You move through the treetops like acrobats. You swing on vines. Abbez somersaults from branch to branch, and Pirate glides along on his brilliant wings. As you proceed, you notice the ground beneath you becoming dry, and the few vines spindly and weak.

At last you must drop to the ground and continue on foot. You thank Abbez for his generous help.

You hear thunder in the distance, but you know it is not the sound of a storm.

You bravely walk forward, Pirate on your shoulder, knowing you travel toward the Fortress of Fray.

Turn to page 99.

10

from page 7

You are alarmed at Caladrius' news. You decide you will be of the most help if you can stop the fighting between Hod, the Wizard of Earth, and Rilla, the Wizardess of Water.

You finish your sweeping and wash the toad dust from your boots. To your relief, the boots reappear.

You enter the wizard's castle and listen for Caladrius. Soon you hear him rattling around his Chamber of Changes. He must be working spells. You quietly climb the great stone staircase that leads to the chamber. Before you even have a chance to knock, the door swings open. Slowly you enter the chamber.

Caladrius steps from a circle of runes he has drawn on the floor. He holds a pouch made of leather patchwork.

"Well, Simon," he says, "you have decided to settle the battle between Earth and Water? A noble plan. And I shall soothe the feelings of Syrrus and Lunay. If we are successful, then angry Fray will be fighting alone. He will have just his own temper to conquer. If we can halt these attacks, we shall hold a Council of Wizards and settle our differences according to Wizard's Law."

You nod in agreement.

"I have packed you a pouch containing four of my finest spells," says Caladrius. "In addition, please take this slumber dart, a specialty of Lunay's." He hands you a slender black tube with a cork in each end. You slip it into your new pouch and tie the pouch to your belt. Caladrius bids you farewell, and you leave the Castle of Changes.

You set off through the forest to the north. As soon as the castle is out of sight, you sit down on a log to look through your pouch. *[There is a list of the spells you find on page 122. Go to that page, then return here.]*

Satisfied with your defenses, you are ready to continue your journey.

If you go to Rilla's riverboat palace, turn to page 47.

If you walk to Hod's underground house, turn to page 14.

12

from page 46

There is no sign of Caladrius, and the storm of Fray's firestones is getting worse. You remember the old saying "Don't burn your candle at both ends." You are not sure what will happen if you follow the instruction on the candle, but you decide the "invisible defense" is the best answer.

You mount the candle on its side on the spiked candle holder, so that you will be able to light both ends. Then you remove a bit of dried moss from the steel tinderbox. Holding the moss against the cool steel, you strike the box with the flint to make a spark. After a few tries the moss catches fire, and you light the wick at each end of the candle.

The candle gives off a golden light. You sit cross-legged on the floor to wait. Outside you see sparks of every color raining on the castle, like brilliant waterfalls of light. It is a wondrous sight. Best of all, it no longer looks like an attack. Where is Fray?

Slowly spinning on the floor, the candle is making a circle of light with its twin flames. It spins faster and faster, and beyond the four windows you see the waterfall of colored sparks become a sparkling mass of glass.

The castle is swallowed in clear crystal. The walls of the High Tower fade and disappear, replaced by reflecting planes of glass. The floor you sit on fizzles out of sight, to become a slippery mirror. There is no longer a garden, a courtyard, or a castle.

You search for your reflection where there once were walls, but all you see is a glint of light where your eyes must be. Otherwise you are completely invisible.

You can still feel your body, and you move like a skater through the walls of glass. You can no longer tell where you are or where you are going. You see only surfaces of color and light that change when you move, yet are endlessly the same.

Although this is beautiful, you really want to escape from this confusing prism.

If you decide to explore further to look for a way out, turn to page 53.

If you want to try one of your spells, turn to page 107.

14

from page 11

Hod has begun making an army of clay to attack Rilla. You decide to try to talk him out of it.

Although there are hours left before nightfall, you are not sure how far it is to Hod's underground house. You travel along the forest path at a steady rate. Strange sculptures decorate the path.

As you reach the crest of a small hill, you spy a slow-moving figure ahead. You step quietly, and he does not turn around. At first you think he is a gnome or a dwarf. But as you creep closer you recognize the pointy, wide-brimmed hat and jaunty garb of a dorkin. He is trudging along the path, carrying a sack over one shoulder. The sack is almost as large as he is.

You try to remember what you have heard about dorkins. They are said to be silly, but very clever. They are rarely seen outside the forest, and you have never met one before.

Caladrius has taught you to be careful when you are in the forest. But dorkins are not dangerous. It would be nice to have company on your journey.

If you catch up with the dorkin, turn to page 72.

If you follow him for a while longer, turn to page 32.

16

You try to remember everything you have heard about the fireproof phoenix and the legendary salamander.

You know that a phoenix is an ancient bird with vivid red and purple feathers. When it grows old, it sets fire to itself, then rises, youthful, from its own ashes. As a phoenix, you would be camouflaged in fire and able to fly on powerful wings.

You turn your thoughts to the salamander, a favorite creature of the castle's alchemists. Not only is the fire salamander safe at the center of a blaze, but its body actually puts a fire out as it moves through the flames. Its body is icy cold, and some say it is poisonous.

You search through your pouch for the vial of dust you need to transform yourself. The rhyme is not included. You must think of a verse to begin the spell.

If you compose a phoenix poem, turn to page 75.

If you choose a salamander spell, turn to page 24.

Too hungry to sleep, you decide to keep walking. You keep catching sight of the moon on the left. There must be a clearing in that direction, you decide, a good place to look for food and shelter for the night. You set off to the left.

It is dusk, and clouds scuttle past the moon, darkening your path. You notice a hazy glow ahead of you. The moon has lit a mossy clearing, bordered on one side by a tiny stream.

You hear a soft, rustling noise as you step into the clearing, but no one is about. You notice a bush laden with ripe, purple berries. You don't recognize the berries, but they don't look like any of the poisonous ones Caladrius has warned you about. You cautiously nibble one. It is juicy and delicious. Your stomach feels fine, you don't shrink or grow, and you are still visible. The berries must be all right. Soon you have eaten a handful.

As you cross the stream for a drink of water, you hear high, fluty laughter. You whirl around, but the clearing is empty. You cup your hands and dip them into the stream. As you drink, the laughter and the voices grow more distinct. You see small points of light circling the clearing. You squint and blink several times as the pin dots of light draw closer. Now they gather around you, hovering in midair.

Oh, no, you think, it must be a fairy ring. You know that most fairies and wood sprites are more playful than dangerous, but they love to keep young humans—even wizards' apprentices—as pets. You'd better not tell them what you really are.

"What enchantment is this?" a voice trills merrily next to your ear. "Is it a giant dragonfly?" chimes a voice just behind you. "Maybe it is a clump of seaweed," giggles another. "Well, whatever it is, it is ours now," says a fourth. "It has eaten our berries and drunk from our stream."

You bolt from the clearing, but *spring!* you bounce off an invisible rubbery wall and land right back in the center of the clearing. You run to another spot, but the unseen barrier stops you again.

The giggles grow. "Since we do not know what it is anyway," chirps a fairy voice, "let us turn it into something we want to play with."

"Yes, yes," a chorus of bubbly voices agrees. "Let us change it to a human baby!" one suggests.

You see the little lights bounce and spin as you feel yourself shrinking. "Hey, wait!" you cry out, as you drop to your hands and knees. You see lovely faces bending over you. You kick your fat legs in the air.

"Waah! Waah!" you cry. All you want is some milk.

THE END

from page 93

Deciding to hurry ahead to Fray's fortress, you leave the clay army plodding behind you.

The sun's first rays wash the forest with warm light. You begin to whistle a cheerful tune. Was that an answering whistle? You stop to listen. You decide it must have been a bird and continue on your way. You hear it again, a low, soft whistle in the distance. Perhaps it's just the wind.

Now the forest is growing darker instead of lighter. Suddenly a fierce wind begins to blow. The trees bend and shake as the wind increases. A storm seems to have come from nowhere, and from all directions at once.

The whistling noise grows loud and sharp. You follow the direction of its piercing sound. Far in the distance, you see the figure of a man in a feathery robe. He is calling to the sky and making broad circles with his arms. A swirling gray cloud appears before him. Syrrus!

You watch as the cloud whistles and lengthens into a cone. It begins to turn around itself, growing larger and tighter. It is moving in your direction. It's a cyclone.

You try to run, but the wind is too strong. You put your head down, cross your arms over your chest, and force yourself forward, but the ground is being sucked backward under your feet.

The cyclone is gaining on you. Trees tear up from their roots and fly swirling into the air. You are swept off your feet, and you feel your body being sucked upward. You tumble over and over, buffeted by the rapidly spiraling wall of wind. You are inside the cyclone!

Suddenly all is still. You must have reached the eye of the cyclone. You can feel yourself being carried along in the whistling cloud. Occasionally a tree or an animal floats by. A bird passes your head, looking frightened and confused.

You try to remain calm, and wonder where you will land. Whom would Syrrus attack with a cyclone? You consider each of your spells in turn, but none is of help to you now.

The cyclone is spinning faster and faster, and you bounce up and down on a cushion of wind. You are suddenly lifted and hurled free of the cyclone. You fly through the air and land, hard, on a bed of leaves. The cyclone whizzes past you, whistling on its way.

You are slightly bruised but otherwise unhurt. You rub a scraped elbow, pick yourself up, and brush the leaves from your clothes.

You are on a forest path, and it looks familiar. You hear water gurgling through the wood ahead of you. You are on the path to Rilla's riverboat. Syrrus must have sent the cyclone against Rilla!

You wonder if Hod's clay army has reached Rilla yet. You decide to warn her.

Turn to page 47.

22

Your simple chores seem so unexciting these days. What you truly want is to try your hand at some real wizardry. You push the spilled toad dust into a pile on the floor and finish rubbing it into each of your boots. Then you rub it everywhere—over your suede trousers, your leather tunic, your face, hands, hair, neck, and ears.

You look for a mirror, to make sure you have covered every spot, and you find your reflection in the workshed window. It's working! You pick up the pieces of the broken bottle and read the label:

TOAD DUST—100% PURE
Invisibility Guaranteed for Fur! Hair! All Tanned Hides!
Warning! Ineffective on living skins, scales, feathers,
vegetables, minerals.

You look at your reflection again. Your boots, trousers, and tunic have disappeared. But *you* are still visible. You still have your linen underwear, but you are bald. And your eyebrows are gone.

Burning with embarrassment, you must decide what to do. You could always make clothes from leaves in the forest.

If you confess your mistake to Caladrius, and ask him to help you get your hair back, turn to page 36.

If you stick to your plan to set out on your own, turn to page 30.

from page 29

You bravely agree to become a messenger for the Council of Caladrius.

"Good," says the old wizard. "Then we must see that you are properly equipped. I have prepared a pouch for you containing four of my finest spells." Caladrius hands you a drawstring bag made of leather patchwork.

"And here is a fifth spell, from me," says Lunay. She slips an object into your pouch, a slender black tube with a cork in each end.

"I shall send Pirate with you as companion and scout," says Caladrius. His huge, rainbow-colored parrot lands on your shoulder with a mighty squawk.

"Now, Simon," says Caladrius, "you must take care, for Fray is powerful and angry. If you fail to summon him to the Wizard's Council, you must not be ashamed, for it is no easy task. If he will not come in peace, you must return to us right away. Fray will follow on his own when he learns we are all together, and we will be ready for his attack."

You leave the castle, with Pirate circling over you in a flurry of color. Caladrius and Lunay watch from the drawbridge. You must take the road to Fray's fortress.

Turn to page 98.

24

from page 16

You slip the little bottle of transformation dust from your pouch and then tie the pouch around your neck so that you, as a salamander, can carry it. You tell Pirate to return to Caladrius if you don't come back from Fray's fortress in one hour. Then you compose a rhyme.

In your mind you picture a shiny red salamander. You concentrate on the image as you sprinkle yourself with the dust of change, chanting aloud:

> *"I can move through raging fire*
> *I spread ice where once was flame*
> *I can quench a blazing pyre*
> *Salamander is my name!"*

You feel yourself growing slender. It doesn't hurt at all. Your clothes fall in a heap on the ground. You are shrinking. Your arms and legs shrivel, but you can balance upright on a long tail. You slither loose of your pouch's leather strap. You are a salamander.

You wonder what to do with your spells. One by one, you try to lift the tubes and bottles with your mouth. They are all too large to carry. You turn toward the fortress and skitter quickly to the lava moat. Here I go, you think, as you wriggle down the embankment into the river of fire. To your relief, heat does not affect you. You begin to swim. The lava freezes as you pass through it!

When you near the fortress wall, you dive to the bottom of the moat. It is as you thought: deep beneath the fortress a passage channels the lava upward once again.

You are sucked up and up, through the core of Fray's fortress, the liquid lava turning to ice behind you. You move faster as you near the top of the fortress, and suddenly you shoot out of an opening into the air.

You bang your head against a metal object and fall back downward onto the now-frozen lava fountain. You look up, wondering what stopped your flight. There stands Fray, grinning as he lowers a cage of fine metal mesh over you.

"I've always wanted a pet salamander!" he gloats.

THE END

Leaving the shed, you enter the castle in order to find Caladrius. You want to tell him that you have decided to stay. As you cross the courtyard, you hear the great door knocker drop against the castle door outside. A single knock reaches through the courtyard. Someone wishes to enter the castle.

Sensing no danger, you decide to see who has knocked. You drag the huge portal open, and as it swings slowly in, a figure collapses at your feet.

It is a young woman, dressed in the rags of a shepherdess. You hear the bleating of a flock of sheep beyond the portal. Bending over the shepherdess, you see her eyelids open briefly, revealing eyes as black as night.

"I am weakened by day," she whispers. "Please fetch Caladrius for me."

But Caladrius has already appeared behind you. You have been preoccupied, and you did not hear his approach. With a casual wave of his hand, Caladrius dims the light in the courtyard. Then he slips a clear lozenge between the woman's pale lips. It looks to you like a simple piece of glass, but as it melts, color returns to her cheeks. She opens her eyes.

"I was expecting you, Lunay," says Caladrius.

"Thank you," she murmurs, her voice rich and low. "I was forced to flee my tower, where because of Fray's magic the sun no longer sets. The constant daylight has drained my strength, so I used the last of my powers to disguise myself and my flock."

You notice that you are surrounded by black sheep. After they have all entered the courtyard, you close the portal.

Lunay rises. Her shepherdess costume lies discarded on the floor, and she wears a gown of sapphire stars. As she hums a short, odd tune, the sheep, too, begin to change. Soon the courtyard is carpeted with clumps of black wool. Roaming in place of the cuddly sheep are a silver wolf, a panther, an owl, a raven, a nighthawk, a winged stallion, a shiny lizard, a lumbering black bear, two creatures you've never seen before, several bats, and a sable.

You are amazed and delighted at this spectacle.

"I am glad you like my friends," says Lunay, "but now we must act quickly, before Fray can do any further harm."

"Your disguise has served you very well, Lunay," says Caladrius. Now he turns to you. "Simon, I have called a Council of the Wizards. Lunay has summoned Hod and Rilla, but now she must rest here. I have contacted Syrrus, and he has agreed to come as well. But no one can reach Fray. There is a lightning field around his fortress, and he hears no signals in his anger. I had planned to send Pirate, my parrot, as messenger.

But if you wish, Simon, *you* shall be my messenger instead. The other wizards will arrive shortly.

"There is danger in going to see Fray. I do not want to deceive you. If you do choose to go, Fray may come to us in peace. If you choose *not* to go, Fray will be lured here by the gathering of his imagined enemies. When he learns we are all here together, he will attack."

If you agree to become a messenger for the Council, turn to page 23.

If you want to stay at Caladrius' castle, turn to page 66.

You are too embarrassed to tell Caladrius that your plan has backfired. Besides, you are ready for an adventure, bald or not, and you know you can make clothes in the forest. You look around the shed for useful tools to take along. You find a ball of twine and a small hunting knife.

Caladrius is out of sight, so you slip out of the shed, hurry through the herb garden, and then sprint across the field that separates the castle from the forest. When you reach the woodland bordering the field, you turn back to look at the Castle of Changes. It is true to its name. From this distance, you can see that the color changes constantly, though there is no single moment when the red switches to blue, or the blue to green. The colors merely deepen, or pale into one another.

As you catch your breath, you hope that Old Rattles won't be too angry when he discovers you've run away.

Continuing into the forest, you come to a rough path, and you decide to follow it.

There isn't another soul in sight, but you decide to make yourself clothes right away, in case you meet someone. Then you can look for a safe place to spend the night.

You come to a patch of tall, lacy ferns. They reach from your ankles to your waist. You sit cross-legged on the forest floor and cut a length of twine long enough to tie around your waist. Then you bind pairs of ferns together at their roots to hang over your new twine belt. Soon you have fashioned a long, green skirt.

At a fork in the path, you notice a mound of mud and sticks. You are not used to wearing ferns. They tickle your legs as you walk.

You investigate, and the mound proves to be a large, upside-down bird's nest, at least four feet across. It must have fallen from a nearby tree.

You turn it over and see that it is empty. You look up, but no birds are visible in the trees overhead. Stuck amid the sticks and mud, and scattered on the ground nearby, are sleek turquoise feathers, a few of them broken. You collect all you can find to make a collar. You fix the longest feathers to fall down your back like a cape, and use the shorter feathers to fringe the tops of your shoulders and ring your chest. Now when you move, you shimmer brilliantly. Perhaps in the forest you will be taken for an elf king.

It has begun to grow dark, and you are hungry. And you need a place to sleep.

If you want to search for food and keep walking until it's completely dark, turn to page 17.

If you prefer to go hungry, and settle in the nest for the night, turn to page 111.

from page 14 / from page 106

You follow the dorkin down the winding path, taking care to stay out of sight. You have traveled almost a mile when the dorkin comes to a halt at a fork in the road. He drops his large sack to the ground, and you duck behind a tree to watch.

The dorkin unties the sack, opens it, and pokes his head inside.

"Juno," he calls. "It's three o'clock. Time to trade."

A yawning lady dorkin emerges from the sack. She stretches and fluffs her hair. She looks annoyed.

"You didn't have to drop me like that!" she snaps. The first dorkin hangs his head. "Well, hurry up, Ridney. Swap places or we'll miss the Dorkin Market." She folds her arms and taps her foot impatiently while Ridney climbs into the sack. Then she ties it closed, heaves it over one shoulder, and marches off down the fork to the right.

Smiling about the two dorkins, you continue on your way. You don't want to go to the Dorkin Market, so you choose the path to the left. The path soon narrows. Darkness is falling.

You pick your way along the path. The ground is rising under your feet, and you realize you are climbing a wooded hill.

You see a faint golden light at the top of the hill

and climb toward it. The trees around you grow sparse, and there is a thick covering of moss beneath your feet.

The ground levels out and the light grows stronger. It seems to be coming from a mossy patch of earth ahead of you.

You reach the glowing light. It shines up through a large window cut into the earth. You lie on your stomach and peer through the glass. There, below you, is the huge figure of Hod. He must make his underground home in the mossy mound you have climbed. You are on his roof!

You watch the wizard at work, a bald, doughy man seated at a potter's wheel. Hod is so absorbed that he doesn't seem to detect your presence. One after another he fashions rude beings of red clay. As each creature is finished, he adds it to the ranks lined up in his workshop. They stare into space, inanimate and patient.

You hear Hod's soft, rumbling laugh.

"Soon, my soldiers, you will know the glories of war. Your clay brothers are already on their way to visit watery Rilla. The soaking showers did not ruin *all* the pits where I dig my clay. Heh, heh."

Your hopes sink. It is too late for talk. Hod's first army is already on its way to attack Rilla.

"Soon, my mud men, you will be even stronger," says Hod. "Like your brothers, you are all made of soft, unfired clay. But *you* I will send to visit Fray. And when Fray unleashes his dragons' breath on you, you will harden and become as strong as rock. My invincible army! Conquerors of Wizards!"

Hod places a final clay soldier on the floor before him. Then he stands, mumbling and chanting in a deep, low voice. His fingers twitch and dance. All at once, each creature jerks and breathes. The newborn soldiers begin to dance and twitch. They are alive!

The earth beneath you trembles, and the golden light splashes over the forest to the south. A portal has opened in the side of Hod's mountain, and a river of clay soldiers spills out into the wood.

From below, you hear Hod's commanding voice. "To Fray! To Fray!"

You wonder if you can reach Rilla in time to warn her of Hod's attack. Perhaps you should try to reach Fray instead, to warn him not to use fire on the unfired clay army.

If you race toward Rilla, turn to page 56.

If you race ahead of the clay army marching on Fray, turn to page 92.

You don't want to spend another hairless minute. Swallowing your pride, you head for the castle to look for Caladrius. Soon you find him shuffling about in the armory. As he catches sight of you, you cringe with embarrassment.

"Hee, hee, hee," he cackles. "Toad dust, eh? Hee, hee! I should tan your hide for you. Then it will work! Hee, hee!"

"Caladrius, sir, change me back, *please*," you say. "I'm sorry. I'll never meddle again. I promise."

"Hee, hee. You look like a plucked goose." His laughter grows quieter. But you see your reflection in a suit of armor and dissolve into a fit of giggles yourself. You *do* look very funny—without any hair on your head, your ears stick out—and soon you are both laughing until tears run down your cheeks.

"Well, my fine little goose," says the wizard, "were you planning to tackle Fray all by yourself? You're a brave one—and foolish, too. The Fire Wizard's powers should command your respect.

"We need a Wizard's Council, before matters can get any worse. I have contacted Hod and Rilla, who have agreed to attend. Lunay is on her way, and she has been able to convince Syrrus to come. But there is a lightning field surrounding Fray's domain, and I have been unable to reach him. I have no choice but to send a messenger.

"I had planned to send my parrot, Pirate. But since you are so willing to risk danger, and so eager to wield spells, I will arm you with wizardry and send *you* instead. That is, if you are willing."

You nod bravely.

"Good. Then we must see you properly equipped. In this pouch you will find four of my finest spells." He hands you a leather drawstring bag. "You will find this blow dart useful. It is a slumber dart, made by Lunay." He gives you a slender black tube with a cork in each end. You put it into your pouch. "And Pirate will go with you as companion and scout." Caladrius' huge, rainbow-feathered parrot lands on your shoulder and makes a series of clucking noises that sound like the bones of his wizard master.

"There is one further matter," says Caladrius, "and that is the toad dust. In order that you do not forget your foolish act, I want you to replace it.

"This magical powder is not made from the skins of just any unfortunate toad. It is collected from the backs of a rare and particularly dusty species of toad found in only the dustiest of places—the attic of a haunting. And the nearest haunted attic is in the Cottage of Caterwaul, five miles from the edge of Fray's domain. If you detour for toad dust, it might prove useful to you in your quest for Fray. But delay may bring disaster in this Wizard's War. Perhaps you should fetch Fray first and postpone your toad hunt until after the council. This is now your journey, and you must use your own judgment.

"As for your baldness, you need only take a bath. Toad dust washes off."

Caladrius stands on the drawbridge and waves good-bye. Pirate circles your head, cawing, "Which way? Which way?"

If you head to the southeast, toward the Cottage of Caterwaul, turn to page 85.

If you set off directly to Fray's fortress in the southwest, turn to page 98.

The hail of firestones grows fierce, and there is no sign of Caladrius. This is an emergency. You place the candle onto the spike in the candle holder. Then you remove a bit of dried moss from the tinderbox and hold it against the cool steel. Striking the box with the flint, you make a spark. In a few tries the moss catches fire, and you light the wick. It ignites with a hiss.

The candle gives off a warm, yellow light. You move away from the center of the room and crouch against a curving wall.

A strand of smoke rises from the flickering candle until it reaches the peak of the beehive ceiling. The hissing sound gets louder. You stare in wonder as the wax begins to spill *upward*. As the wick burns merrily, the candle lengthens and stretches, following the path of the thin column of smoke as it rises to the ceiling. When it can grow no further, the candle fastens itself to the center of the ceiling, a waxen rope, its flame extinguished.

For a moment all is quiet, except for the rain of firestones outside. Suddenly you are shaken by a rumbling in the stone walls of the High Tower. You know it is not an earthquake—the walls are vibrating, but the floor is not. You throw yourself flat on the floor.

Now, terrified, you see the reason for the shaking. The stone beehive, with a great, ripping sound, is separating itself from the wooden floor of the High Tower and rising into the air! A space opens around you where once there were walls.

The beehive is now hovering three feet above the floor, and the brass candle holder is dangling in the air by its rope of wax.

You climb down into the trapdoor but continue to watch through the opening.

The wax rope begins to swing from the ceiling. It swings wider and wider, until the brass candle holder strikes a wall with a spark and a ringing *gong!* The tower has become an enormous bell, with the candle holder its clapper. *Gong, gong!* The clapper swings and the bell tower sounds its alarm.

A buzzing echo rings in your ears. The buzzing gathers force. You watch in amazement as each flying spark from the striking clapper changes into a buzzing bee. Soon there is an angry swarm, flying in formation beneath the beehive bell.

Without waiting another minute, you run down the spiral staircase to find Caladrius. He is standing in the courtyard with a fireproof umbrella.

"Now watch this," he says with a wink. "This is the best part!"

You look to the sky and see Fray, riding on clouds of smoke, ready to drive a lightning bolt at your feet.

"Surrender, Caladrius!" he roars, red-faced in fury. Then he howls in pain and slaps his arm. He drops his lightning bolt, which clatters harmlessly to the ground, and slaps his wrist. Caladrius' army of bees form a buzzing line and encircle him from neck to toe. Binding him in a chain of bees, they drag him to the courtyard on a leash.

You hear laughter behind you, and turn to see Syrrus and Rilla, Hod and Lunay enter the courtyard from the castle beyond.

"We came to meet with Caladrius," says Lunay. "We were in conference when Fray attacked, and ready to engage him in battle, but Caladrius just gave a wave of his hand and said, 'Simon will handle it.'"

"B-but..." you stammer, wondering how Caladrius knew you were there.

"You acted bravely and well, Simon," says Hod. "Caladrius should be proud." Syrrus and Rilla nod in agreement.

You feel Fray staring at you, and turn to face him. He looks like a mummy, wrapped in bees.

"Are you the one called Simon?" he barks. You nod. "I have been outbattled by a mere apprentice?"

"It was Caladrius' candle—" you start to explain, but the old wizard pokes his elbow into your side, so you hold your tongue.

"Outdone by an *apprentice!*" Fray says gruffly. "Well, I guess Supreme Wizard is not the job for me after all. I would say Supreme Fool is more like it!" He chuckles. The bees buzz with laughter and unravel their lines. Fray stops laughing and thoughtfully strokes his mustache. "To the conference table?" he says.

"To the conference table!" answer the wizards.

Caladrius rests a hand on your shoulder. "We would be most honored, Simon," he says proudly, "if you would join us."

THE END

You find Caladrius in the armory and tell him you have decided to set off on your own. The wizard gives you a sturdy leather pouch filled with spells. He wishes you luck and bids you a fond farewell.

You walk to the edge of the forest, and as soon as you are out of sight of the castle, you sit down on a tree stump to look through the pouch. *[There is a list of what you find on page 122. Please go to that page, then return.]*

You put your spells back into the pouch and wait until the daylight begins to fade. Then you steal silently back into Caladrius' castle and sneak to the winding stone staircase that leads to the High Tower. You intend to keep watch and to help defend the castle against Fray if you must.

You climb and climb the spiraling stairs, resting against the cool stone walls when you get dizzy. At the top of the stairs you come to a round trapdoor over your head. You push it open and pull yourself into the room above. Then you replace the trapdoor in the floor and look around you.

You are in the center of a tiny, round room. The walls and ceiling, made of thick stone blocks, arch above you like a beehive. Four narrow slits, facing north, south, east, and west, shed rosy light on the plank floor.

The only furnishings in this curious room are a crude but sturdy wooden table and chair. There is a thick white candle on the table, with an irregular pattern worked into it. The pattern appears to be lettering, but it is hard to make out. You scrape some dried mud off the soles of your boots and crumble the pieces into a fine brown powder. Then you roll the candle in the dirt until you can read the carved letters in white against a darker background:

CANDLE OF CALADRIUS

In case of an emergency
Place and burn me centrally.

For an invisible defense,
Burn this candle at
both ends.

Next to the candle you find a steel tinderbox, a flint, and a brass candle holder with a small spike for affixing the candle.

You puzzle over the verses. What kind of emergency? What will happen? Where is "centrally"? What will become invisible? The High Tower? The entire castle?

You examine the tower room once again. The center of the circle made by the trapdoor is directly beneath a circular stone at the peak of the beehive ceiling. This must be the spot where you should place the candle.

It is growing dark, so you position the candle holder at the center of the room. Next to it you place the tinderbox and the candle, so you will be able to find them in the dark. You are ready. All is quiet. How will you be able to lift the trapdoor if you burn the candle? You nervously hum a song.

Suddenly the room is light again with an orange glow. Looking out the southern window, you see a whirling fireball blaze past your tower and land in the herb garden with a thunderous roar. Fray is attacking!

"What will Caladrius do?" you wonder. Another fireball hurtles toward the drawbridge.

You hear a rumbling laugh from afar, the threatening laugh of Fray. You begin to smell smoke. A lightning bolt crackles past the west window and strikes a stone wall in the courtyard.

Now it is raining flames, spattering the castle roofs and towers with a hail of firestones. Caladrius is silent.

You cannot see Fray, but you know he must be close. Where is Caladrius, the Wizard of Changes?

If you wait for Caladrius to appear, turn to page 80.

If you burn the candle at both ends, turn to page 12.

If you decide it's an emergency, turn to page 39.

You follow the woodland path toward Rilla's riverboat palace. The path runs beside a pleasant stream. The stream soon widens to a rushing river, and Rilla's riverboat rises into view. It is a magnificent palace, floating on the sparkling water.

You see a figure standing on the shore. It doesn't look like one of Hod's clay soldiers, and you see no sign of the army of clay. You draw closer and see that it is the Wizardess of Water herself.

Rilla is dressed in a gown of shimmering fish scales studded with sparkling seashells and coral. She blows a stream of small bubbles from her mouth, which float over the water and pop on the surface of the river. As each bubble pops, shining fish with fins like wings leap from the water and glint in the sun. Soon the water is stirred into a frenzy of leaping fish.

Rilla's voice calms the frothing waters, and the fish await her words in the lapping waves.

"Greetings, my friends, my flying fish!" she says in a melodious voice. "My enemy Syrrus, Wizard of Air, has sent a cyclone to destroy my palace, but I have sailed my palace beyond its path."

You can see the gap that the cyclone cut through the forest several yards away. Rilla speaks again.

"Now Syrrus may send his army of strongbirds to attack me—but you shall surprise them in battle, my flying fish. We shall attack first!"

You are beginning to grow angry and worried. You would like to help, but the war is getting worse. None of your spells seems to be of any use here.

You are not far from Lunay's Tower of Stars. Perhaps you should appeal to her for help in stopping the armies of strongbirds and flying fish. Or perhaps Rilla will hold back her attack on Syrrus if you tell her an army is coming from Hod.

If you want to tell Rilla about Hod's clay army, turn to page 94.

If you want to try to get help from Lunay, turn to page 56.

You cup your hands around your mouth and shout at the top of your voice. "Oh, great Fire Wizard, hear me, Fray! I come with a message from Caladrius. Let me enter and speak with you."

A sizzling bolt of lightning sears the gray earth at your feet. You try again.

"Hear me, Fray, and let me enter. There is to be a Council of Wizards. Your attendance is requested."

A furious voice thunders from the metal walls of the fortress. "No one shall enter the Fortress of Fray! I take no orders from apprentices. Begone, before I open your grave in the ground you stand on!"

You retreat from the fortress and consider your choices.

If you use your transformation spell, turn to page 16.

If you return to Caladrius' castle to attend the Council, turn to page 66.

from page 87

You draw Lunay's slumber dart from your pouch and slowly open the attic door.

"EEEeeeyiiiIII!" The angry banshee whisks toward you. A shiver of terror passes through you, but you remember your purpose. Every hair on your body is standing at attention as you fall to one knee and bow deeply.

"Oh, Great Prince," you say in as strong a voice as you can muster. "I have heard your tortured song and bring you a gift of the sleep you crave."

The banshee has stopped in mid-shriek. You watch as he assumes the form of a ghostly prince. He listens in silence as his eyes fill with icy tears.

"They call me Simon the Guardian," you continue. "I offer you sweet dreams, and in return for your hospitality I will gladly guard your toads while you rest." At the mention of his precious toads, the ghost's sorrowful expression turns to suspicion. You speak quickly. "If you will allow me to say so, Your Highness, you do not look well. I daresay that few of your visitors understand the strain of your work."

The banshee prince answers you in a distant voice. "It is true, so *true*, he moans. "These centuries of sleep-lessness have made me—sooo crannnky. I am eeeager to sleeeeep, and I accept your offer, Guardiannnn. Maybeeee when I wake, we can sing together, and I shall tell you my liiife storyyyy."

"I shall be honored to hear it, sire," you reply, bowing deeply again. "Now, please observe my rare slumber wand." You grip the dart firmly and uncork the end marked "blow."

"I must whisper to it," you explain, and put the open end to your lips. The banshee lunges forward to grab the magic dart. Pirate squawks. You wait until you are nearly engulfed by the banshee, then quickly uncork the end marked "dart" and blow as hard as you can.

The dart passes through the banshee and lodges in the wall. The foggy prince falls at your feet, sound asleep. The room fills with noise—the banshee's snores and the croaks of toads. The slumber dart has done its work.

Picking up the empty tube, you and Pirate corner fat toads and sweep the dust from their backs into the tube. When the tube is full, you cork both ends.

Moonlight beams through a hole in the ceiling, creating a dancing patch of light on the floor. You yawn with exhaustion. You really need some sleep. The prince is dreaming deeply, but you don't know how long the spell will last. And there may be other dangers in this haunted cottage. On the other hand, you would have to make your way through the moonlit swamp outside before you could find a dry place to sleep in the forest.

If you want to sleep in the cottage, turn to page 64.

If you decide to cross the swamp, turn to page 81.

You begin to explore the mirrored maze. You glide through a panel of icy blue and are faced with six more identical walls. You call for Caladrius, but your voice makes no sound. You move onward, through pane after pane of jellylike colors. There is no end in sight. You pass through countless layers of tinted tinsels until you notice the colors growing paler.

Looking back, you can make out, far in the distance, the twin specks of light from the spinning candle. The flames are getting closer together as the candle melts.

Ahead of you the glassy walls grow clearer yet, and you can see the filmy shapes of trees, oddly round and wavering, as though you were looking through the eyes of a fish. It is the forest that borders Caladrius' castle. There must be a way out! You move toward the trees.

You reach the last crystal wall, a thin, transparent curve. You see the forest beyond as if you were inside a huge soap bubble.

A shadow falls over the forest, and Fray emerges, angrily searching the space in front of him. Striding straight toward you, he bangs into the crystal wall and rubs his bruised nose as he peers ahead of him. He presses his whole body against the invisible barrier, his face squashed and terrible, like a face mashed against a window. He is separated from you by the thinnest of barriers.

You timidly poke a finger through the curving wall. It passes through easily and becomes visible beyond the barrier. You tickle Fray in the belly.

Fray hollers and grabs for your finger, but you pull it back behind your crystal wall. It disappears again. It seems that you can get out of the maze but Fray cannot get in.

Behind you, you can see that the candle has almost burned out. You feel a wave of panic. You are afraid that you will be trapped forever inside this maze of glass, once the candle is gone.

Fray is plastered against the crystal wall again, searching for an opening. You reach through the wall, grab his wrist, and yank as hard as you can. His arm passes into the maze, attached to your own. You keep a firm hold and yank again.

Fray's body comes hurtling through the barrier. His own weight sends him tumbling behind you. He steadies himself and rises to his feet—fully visible—but he stops to shade his sight against the brilliant specks of light that are all he can see of your eyes.

The candle in the distance begins to flicker. You dive through the crystal wall to the forest outside, just as the candlelight goes out.

You rub your eyes. It is dawn, and you are visible again! You are standing at the edge of the forest.

Caladrius' castle rises before you, and the wizard himself stands at your side.

"Simon, have you slept in the forest all night?" asks Caladrius. "You know that can be dangerous. Ahhh, but you have found my crystal ball! I thought I had lost it for good."

You look down at your feet. There lies Caladrius' crystal. The old wizard scoops it up off the ground and pops it into its black velvet carrying bag.

But you grin to yourself as you both make your way back to the castle. Just as the crystal ball disappeared into the bag, it caught a ray of the morning sun. Deep inside, you saw the tiny figure of Fray, shaking his fists and hammering to be let out. Maybe you and Caladrius will let him out soon, if he promises to be peaceful. You have ended the War of the Wizards.

THE END

56

from page 35 / from page 48

Entering the forest, you begin to run. The War of the Wizards is growing, and you have not been able to do anything to stop it.

You run with the wind howling at your back. Where is the wind coming from? Suddenly you notice that something else is wrong. The forest has become as dark as night, yet you can still see. Flashes of lightning zigzag above the leafy forest ceiling. You think you see a ball of fire, or maybe a comet.

The wind pushes you to the top of a ridge overlooking a valley. You see that you are too late. The valley has become a battlefield.

You grab hold of a tree as the wind rushes past you. Syrrus, the Wizard of Air, riding on the wind's tail, howls like a storm. He swoops into the valley and blows out a blazing wall of fire as if it were a candle. But Syrrus' wind is stopped by Hod's mud soldiers, who have been hardened to walking rocks by Fray's fire.

All at once the rock soldiers tumble like rows of tenpins as a geyser splits the earth beneath them, spurting high into the air. Rilla's voice cries in triumph, "Water will win!"

Now you see Hod, directing his army from a grove of oaks. With an angry grunt, he wrenches a towering tree from the ground and staggers a bit under its weight.

Then he carries it, roots dangling, to the steaming geyser and plants it, leaves first, in the spraying hole. The geyser is plugged. But the rest of the oaks are being ripped from their roots by Syrrus' cyclone. And now Fray sets the trees on fire. The trees fly through the air like burning spears, aimed at the spot where Rilla's laugh came from. But they land with a hiss in a pool of water, and the battle rages on.

The valley is in chaos. Armies of ferocious birds, dragons, mud men, and flying fish clash on land and in the air. The noise is so great you can barely think as you watch from the safety of the ridge.

You search the valley for a sign of Caladrius, but he is nowhere to be seen. Nor can you find the Wizardess of Night, Lunay. You hope they are safe together at the Castle of Changes, and you wonder what to do.

If you let the wizards battle it out, they may destroy each other. They will certainly destroy the Forgotten Forest.

You must find a spell that will help—but which one? Even if you put one wizard to sleep with your slumber dart, change another into a termite, and shrink a third, there would still be a war when the spells wore off. You wish that you could explain things to them. But you would have to be a giant before they would listen to you. A giant!

If you were larger than the valley below you, no mere lightning bolts or winds or waters could hurt you. Dragon bites would feel like mosquito bites, and mud men would be flattened under your feet.

You decide the growing spell is your only chance. You reach for the little black bottle in your pouch and pour half of the inky liquid into your right hand. You slap the liquid onto your hair and wait. Nothing happens. You empty the bottle into your right hand and splash the liquid onto your head.

You hear a loud cracking. It is the ridge you are standing on. You are so large it will no longer hold your weight!

A single step brings you to the center of the valley. You lean down and pluck Hod from a nearby tree and drop him into your shirt pocket. You reach out and grip Syrrus as he flees in a blast of wind. The wind is just a gentle breeze to you, and you tuck the wizard into your belt. You dip into a roaring river, a shallow puddle to you, and capture Rilla. You must hold her firmly, as she is slippery and tries to wriggle from your hand. Finally you grasp Fray by the seat of his pants and haul him into the air.

You speak to the four wizards in your deep, giant's voice. "Look below you at the valley you have destroyed. This fighting must stop. You have *equal* powers, all of

you, and you need one another as well. Hod needs water and fire to mold his clay, and water and air to grow herbs. Rilla must have earth through which her rivers can flow, sky in which to rain, heat to keep her water from freezing. Likewise, Syrrus, you need the others. And, Fray, without air your fires cannot burn.

"You are deeply respected in the forest as the great powers you are. But you must respect one another, and help those weaker than yourselves."

You can see that the wizards are ashamed, and you lower them to the ground. At your feet stands Lunay! She invites each wizard to a Council of Wizards at the Castle of Changes. They all agree to go.

You hear a rattling on your shoulder and a voice in your ear.

"You are indeed a giant, Simon," says Caladrius proudly. "And a giant you shall remain, even after I shrink you back to normal size. For you have brought peace to the Forgotten Forest!"

THE END

from page 7

You splash some water on your boots and they reappear.

As you finish your sweeping, you think about the War of the Wizards. You have lived in Caladrius' castle for a long time, and you have shared many adventures with him. You decide to stand by your master. What wizardry will he use against Fray, the Wizard of Fire? You are eager to learn new wonders, for Caladrius is always at his best when danger is near.

But what if the old wizard does not want you to stay? Does he think you will be in the way? Or does he really need your help? And what about the spells he offered you? You are not sure what to do.

If you accept Caladrius' spells and pretend to leave, but then hide somewhere in the castle until you can be of help, turn to page 44.

If you find Caladrius and tell him you are staying, turn to page 26.

The banshee prince is snoring peacefully, his toads croaking in reply. Hoping he will sleep for hours, you decide to spend the rest of the night in the Cottage of Caterwaul. With the parrot behind you, you tiptoe down the attic steps.

You are in a long, narrow corridor. On one side a railing separates you from the central hallway and the lower floors. On the other side of the corridor are three doors, each lit by candelabra that drip white wax onto the floor.

You grab a candle and slowly open the first door. You jump as you see a ghostly patch of white, but it is just a linen closet filled with mildewed sheets.

The second door leads to a small library. You run your fingers along a row of books. The leather bindings feel clammy, like wet lizards. You feel something dragging on your boot—a piece of seaweed? What you thought was a floral pattern in the carpet turns out to be algae of some sort. An inviting armchair faces a fireplace at one end of the room, but as you draw closer you can see that jagged springs have worked their way through its seat.

You decide to try the third door. Back in the corridor you hear a faint sound from the lower floors, a soft lapping, like the sound of a kitten drinking milk. The third door opens into a master bedroom. In the center of the room stands a huge, canopied bed. There are draped and shuttered windows on either side. You climb onto the bed to test the mattress. Pirate perches at the foot of the bed to keep watch. You don't care if the bed is not perfectly dry. You leave your candle on the nightstand next to the bed and drop off to sleep.

You are jolted awake with a sense of danger. The lapping noise you heard earlier has grown louder. It is now a sucking, gurgling sound. *Slurp. Slurp.* It seems to be coming from everywhere at once.

You hop out of bed. Just as your feet hit the floor, the bed canopy collapses with a crash! You have narrowly escaped being crushed.

The floor feels slimy as you run to a window. You pull back the curtains and throw open the shutters, expecting to see the forest beneath you. You see a muddy lagoon. *Slurp. Slurp.* The water is almost level with the bottom of the window, and it is rising. Or the house is sinking!

"Pirate, let's go!" you cry, and run back into the corridor. The lower floors of the house are under water. The soupy pool has almost reached your level. An ax flies past your nose and lands with a thud in the wall. Something is trying to make sure you don't leave the Cottage of Caterwaul. You think fast.

If you decide to swim for it and search for a way out, turn to page 71.

If you try to escape through the attic, turn to page 88.

66

You can't be sure that you can convince Fray to attend the Council of Wizards, so you join with Caladrius and Lunay in the courtyard and wait for the other wizards to arrive. You do not have to wait for long.

Hod, the Wizard of Earth, arrives first, plodding along on a dusty plow horse, spattered with mud from his journey.

Next, Syrrus sweeps in with a gust of air that sends Hod's dust flying and the balls of black wool rolling into a corner.

Finally Rilla comes and releases a refreshing spray that sprinkles the courtyard and washes the mud from tired Hod.

"Wizards all," says Caladrius, "I welcome you to my Castle of Changes. Let us go at once to the Council Chamber to talk of change for the better." He turns to you. "Simon, please get food and drink for Lunay's flock, and then stand guard outside the chamber door. Interrupt us only if Fray should appear."

You follow Caladrius' order and settle down in front of the heavy door to the Council Chamber. Lunay's friends munch happily around you, except for the bats, who hang upside down, asleep. The lizard drapes himself across your shoulder, and the silver wolf lies at your feet.

You press your ear to the door, but it is too thick and you can hear nothing of the conference inside.

You wander to the window next to the great door. The window opens onto a cloudless sky. When you look down, you can see the fields that surround the castle and, beyond, the edge of the forest.

After a time you hear raised voices in the Council Chamber, and you press your ear to the door once more.

"I must control all things that fly!" declares Syrrus.

"But not my flying fish!" says Rilla.

"Nor my winged horse," adds Lunay.

"My parrot? My flying carpet?" says Caladrius.

Then everyone begins to talk at once, until Lunay's warm voice sings a soothing lullaby and all grows calm once again. You wonder if they have fallen asleep, but soon the squabbling voices return.

You hear a small storm outside, but whether it is a rainshower of Rilla's or one of Syrrus' cyclones, or even an earthquake of Hod's, you cannot tell. It passes quickly, and there is silence once again.

Outside, the sun is setting beyond the fields, glazing the sky a pale orange. As the sun falls into the forest, the color deepens to a flaming red and you hear a crackling laugh above you. There you see the dark silhouette of Fray against the blazing sky. He calls to you:

"When the sky has burnt to ashy black
        Then, tell your friends, Fray will attack!"

And then you see nothing but smoke.

You pound on the door of the Council Chamber, shouting, "Fray will attack at nightfall! Fray will attack tonight!" There is no answer, and it is starting to get dark.

You are sure the wizards have heard you. But it is strangely quiet inside. Are they planning their battle strategy?

If you enter the Council Chamber to find out, turn to page 82.

If you plan a battle strategy of your own, turn to page 118.

You lie on the tree limb to rest until morning. The ghostly noises in the Cottage of Caterwaul gradually ebb, and you doze off.

You awaken to a collection of croaks. You are surrounded by giant toad warriors! They line the tree limb and cover the rooftop.

One of them is wearing your pouch as a hat. Another is pouring your toad dust back through the hole in the cottage roof. A third has cast your inverse ointment into the swirling lagoon beneath you, while a fourth has shrunk several of his companions by mistake. A fifth wears your mirror amulet, to no effect, as his friends continue to view him as a toad warrior like themselves. And a sixth is sprinkling a fine dust over your head and croaking what you fear may be a toadish rhyme.

You try to shake the dust from your hair, but it is too late. All you can do is croak in dismay.

THE END

from page 65

Slurp. Slurp. The Cottage of Caterwaul continues to sink. You don't want to run into the banshee in the attic again, so you decide to try to swim out of the house. The water has almost reached a row of windows opposite you, at the front of the house. You will have to swim across the vast hallway—now a swampy pool—to reach them. You don't like the look of the muddy water. It seems to be drinking the house, smacking its lips with each thirsty swallow. *Slurp.*

You are glad it's not far to the windows. Pirate has flown safely across the hallway and has started to hammer at a window with his beak, the water already soaking his tail feathers. You climb over the corridor railing, drop into the pool, and begin to swim toward Pirate.

You are not alone in the pool. Something eely whips by your cheek. Weedy tendrils brush your legs and arms. The water grows choppy and then begins to churn. You try to swim harder, but you are moving in circles. It's a whirlpool! You try to call to Pirate, but your mouth fills with water. As you spin faster and faster, you are dragged down into the center of the whirlpool.

You hear the banshee's shrieking laughter, and remember how dry it was in the attic, as you are sucked underwater. *Slurp. Slurp.*

THE END

from page 14

You like company, and you decide to catch up with the dorkin. "Hello!" you call.

The dorkin turns his head and winks. "Hello, yourself!" he answers in a friendly voice. "My name is Ridney. It seems we are traveling in the same direction. Where are you going?"

"I am Simon the Apprentice, and I hope to reach the wizard Hod. Is this the right road?"

"Yes, but you must walk many miles yet," replies the dorkin. "I'm on my way to the Dorkin Market—to bargain, trade, and barter. That's what dorkins do, you know. We swap. We trade treasures."

He eyes your pouch casually and continues to chat. "It's an ancient custom. It's considered very rude to refuse to trade with a dorkin, you know. We make exchanges large and small, little or all. We own what we own while we own it, and we always have something new. We pass on our most precious possessions." He wags a finger at you. "Dorkins are not greedy hoarders! *Our* valuables are used and admired. We never store them in a vault or a cave, like *some!*" The dorkin sniffs scornfully.

You are a bit taken aback by this remark, but you think of the way gnomes and dwarves hoard their treasures in hidden caverns where no one can enjoy them.

"It seems like a very good idea," you say politely. You realize that you are making slow progress now as the dorkin struggles with his heavy sack. "Is it far to the Dorkin Market?" you ask.

"It is close," says the dorkin. "Less than a mile. But my bulky burden slows me down. If you would be so kind as to carry it for me a short way, I would be glad to hold your leather pouch."

You sense a trick, and you are not about to be laden with his heavy sack while he skips away with your spells. "Let's rest awhile instead," you suggest, and seat yourself on the side of the road. The dorkin unshoulders his weighty sack and happily sits beside you.

"I'll bet you are curious to know what's in this sack of mine," says the dorkin with a grin. "I'll swap you the whole thing for that little pouch of yours."

You were afraid he was leading up to such an offer.

"Oh, no, I couldn't do that," you answer quickly.

He looks a bit insulted at your refusal. Then he shrugs.

"I can see that you do not value the honor of trading with a dorkin," says Ridney. "But you are young and inexperienced. I will make you a more generous offer, to teach you the value of trading. If you will give me just one item from that pouch of yours, I will give you my sack. But you must trade me the first thing your hand touches when you reach into your pouch."

You hesitate. His sack is heavy enough to contain a great deal of gold or jewelry. You would not want to carry such a weight on your journey, but you could bury it in the forest and return for it later. You would lose only one spell. But which one? And what if the dorkin's sack is full of rocks? Or sand? It didn't rattle or make any noise.

You want to be on your way, but you hate to be rude.

If you agree to the dorkin's swap, turn to page 108.

If you refuse and take your leave, turn to page 106.

Studying the little vial of transformation dust, you wonder what it will feel like to change into something else. First you remember to tie your pouch around your neck. Then you tell Pirate to wait for you outside the fortress and to return to Caladrius if you don't come back in one hour.

You shut your eyes and picture a phoenix as clearly as you can. You remove the stopper from the vial and concentrate on your mental image of a large, long-necked bird as you sprinkle the glittering dust over your head and recite your rhyme:

> *"I wish to be immune to flame*
> *And take the Phoenix as my name,*
> *So when I speak the magic word*
> *Transform me to this firebird!"*

Suddenly your clothes are bursting, your boots are splitting, and feathers sprout from your skin. Claws form at your feet, your mouth stretches and hardens into a pointy beak, your eyesight grows keen, and where you once had shoulder blades you now possess great wings. The change happened so quickly that you felt no pain. You are now a phoenix, with feathers the colors of mulberries and roses. Your pouch rests on your chest, suspended from the cord around your neck. You are ready.

Lifting your wings, you rise into the air. You decide to circle Fray's fortress, starting at its base, until you find an entrance. It is wonderful to fly! You wish you could forget the dark fortress before you and fly away on your strong new wings.

The last rays of the sun turn your feathers to shimmering satin. Below you, blackened craters pit the earth. You focus your attention once more on the lava-streaked fortress.

As you near the streams of lava you feel a red-hot glow begin within your body. Its heat matches that thrown by the lava, but the burning does not hurt you at all. You fly in a spiral, up and around the fortress, searching for the source of the lava flow. The narrow slits open and close in the solid walls of the fortress as you pass. You suspect they are magical illusions and that you would be crushed if you tried to fly through one.

At the peak of the fortress you reach the cone-shaped tower. It has a circular opening at its top, like the mouth of a volcano. You see that the tower is hollow at the center, with a tube of platforms and staircases snaking downward into darkness. Ringing this tube are the lava channels, drawn upward from the moat far below, just as you suspected. And standing on the uppermost platform, open to the sky, is Fray. He has not seen you yet.

Anchoring your claws at the top of a lava channel, you overlook Fray's platform. You blend perfectly with the fiery lava, and your head licks above the wall of the channel like a single flame. You will be able to hide and watch until you decide what to do next.

Fray stands proudly just below you, his scarlet hair whipped back from his face. He wears fine armor and a vest of chain mail. In outstretched hands he grips his most famous weapons, a frightening pair of fire torches. The torches cast a lasso of flame in an arc that frames his head.

"Where are my enemies?" he demands in a thunderous voice. "They have fled before me like mice. Syrrus! Caladrius! Rilla!" he bellows. "Come to me. I shall prove my power over this land!"

At this boast you angrily forget your plan. Does he not see the destruction he has caused?

"You have *burned* the land!" you cry, as you emerge like a living flame from your hiding place.

Fray roars in fury and heaves one of the torches at you. It pierces your leather pouch of spells, which bursts into flames. You can feel the torch burn you as Fray reels you toward him on his fiery rope. Your body burns into ashes, and all goes dark.

Suddenly, you hear him shriek, "What Fire Wizard is this?" You are rising from the flames, strong and youthful, a newborn phoenix. The fire torch pinned the mirror amulet to your chest. Now Fray sees you as another wizard.

Full of new strength, you grasp Fray by the shoulders in your purple talons. Then you lift your great wings and carry him off into the night, your path lit by the weakening fire torch, Fray hanging helpless and terrified in your claws.

"Now look down," you command, "and see the damage your foolishness has done. You have turned the greenery to ashes. You have wasted your powers in useless display. But as I have sprung from the ashes, beautiful and young, so can you make new beauty grow here. You will need the help of Syrrus and Rilla, of Hod and Lunay. If you refuse to unite with the Council of Caladrius, and to make amends for the chaos you have caused, you will be stripped of your powers and banished from the Forgotten Forest."

Together you soar on strong wings toward Caladrius' castle, a shame-faced Fray your sorry passenger.

"You speak the truth, Apprentice," Fray admits. "I have done grave wrongs. But from this day forward there will be no more war among the wizards."

THE END

80

Lightning bolts, fireballs, and flame pellets batter the castle. You decide to wait for Caladrius to appear.

Caladrius remains silent as the attack continues. But you are able to calculate Fray's position from the angles of his fiery missiles. He must be standing on top of the High Tower, directly over your head!

Maybe this *is* an emergency. An "invisible defense" may do you no good if Fray is already on the tower. But you can still burn Caladrius' candle.

Or you could use one of your spells. The slumber dart? No, he is not close enough. You can't reach him with any of your ointments or powders, either. You could use the transformation spell on yourself—but what can you turn yourself into that could conquer Fray? You remember the old saying "Fight fire with fire." You would have to change yourself into a fire-breathing dragon to battle with Fray.

If you decide to burn the candle, turn to page 39.

If you want to battle Fray as a dragon, turn to page 84.

You don't care if your feet get wet— you're not spending one more minute in this creepy cottage. You run down the stairs two at a time, Pirate flapping after you, and burst through the front door to the marshy path outside. Hearing a loud, glurping sound, you turn back and see the Cottage of Caterwaul sinking rapidly into the surrounding swamp. The swamp is quicksand —and it seems to be hungry.

You are not safe yet. The path you are standing on slants toward the cottage, and you can feel yourself slipping downward in the muck. You fight your instinct to panic and look quickly around you. You spot a tall tree nearby with an overhanging limb you think you can reach. The treetop looks safe.

If you pull yourself out of the muddy marsh and swing up onto the tree limb, turn to page 103.

If you stay where you are, it's THE END.

82

from page 68

To make sure that the wizards hear your warning, you throw open the door to the Council Chamber. The room is dim—and it is empty.

A highly polished table takes up much of the chamber. The chairs around it are neatly pushed in at their places. There are no windows and no other doors.

You hear Lunay's panther growl. You whip your head around and see the grinning form of Fray blocking the doorway. Your heart thumps wildly as you catch sight of the dagger of sparks in Fray's hand. There is a bulky chair in your way, and you can't get under the table. There is nowhere to hide.

"This is for you, Apprentice!" bellows Fray, and he hurls the dagger.

It lands in the center of the table. Around the sparkling dagger grows a huge pink cake. The little sparks light hundreds of candles on the cake, and the other wizards materialize.

"*Surprise!*" they all cry out at once.

"Do you really think we would fight one another?" says Rilla, laughing. "We just wanted to surprise you."

You cannot stay angry at their scary trick, because they are all smiling and clapping their hands. The cake looks delicious. Your name is written in icing, in fancy script. You begin to laugh.

And then the wizards sing, "Happy Birthday to You."

THE END

from page 107

You decide to try your growing spell. You find the bottle in your pouch. But it, too, is invisible, and you hope you can remember the instructions. *Throw me twice from your right hand*, you think.

You pour half of the liquid into your right hand and splash it onto your head. Dripping, you repeat the process with the rest of the liquid.

Suddenly the bottle feels like a marble. Then it feels like a tiny pebble. You must be growing!

But the maze still shimmers around you.

You try to move through a glowing wall of light. It will not give way. Turning around, you press in every direction, but to no avail.

Now you are enormous, invisible, and lost. And stuck.

THE END

84

from page 80

You turn the bottle of transformation dust over in your hand.

You shut your eyes tightly and picture a huge, red, fire-breathing dragon. You think of a rhyme:

Abba raxus arma gaddon,
Change me to a fighting dragon!

Then you sprinkle yourself with the dust and wait.

You feel yourself growing larger and larger. Your skin hardens and turns to scales. You sprout long claws and a snout. Your serpent's tail shoots out the east window of the tower. Your great bulk crushes the candle beneath you. You cough, and smoke comes out your nose. Then you roar, and a burning flame pours from your mouth. You thrash wildly, but you are too big to get out of the tower. You are trapped!

Your head presses against the west window. You can see Fray outside, riding on twin dragons as large as you.

You hope Caladrius does something soon.

THE END

from page 38

___

You decide you'll need all the help you can get, and a supply of toad dust may come in handy for your journey to see Fray.

You set off toward the Cottage of Caterwaul, with Caladrius' pouch of spells tied securely to your belt and Pirate perched on your shoulder. Before you travel any farther, you sit down on a tree stump to examine your spells. *[There is a list of what you find on page 122. Go to that page and then return.]*

You put the spells back into your pouch and continue on your way.

It is dusk as you near Caterwaul. The terrain has grown quite marshy.

The cottage is creepy: a hollow ruin, half sunken in mire and overgrown with unhealthy-looking vines. Something—probably a bat—suddenly flies from a hole in the roof. You notice a flickering light in what must be the attic. You wonder which of your spells will work against a ghost as you nervously climb the splintered steps to the cottage.

As you step into the gloom, the wooden floorboards creak and the house seems to sink a little further into the boggy mud.

You are in a lofty hall. A rickety staircase leads to the upper floors. As you climb, Pirate digs his claws tightly into your shoulder.

At the top of the stairs, you hear a mournful voice singing in the attic. Its solemn song is accompanied by a

chorus of croaks—the chant of a tribe of toads. You press your ear against the attic door to make out the words:

> I lived a prince,
> But die we must. *(Croak!)*
> Now I'm custodian of the dust. *(Croak!)*
>
> These sleepless nights
> I wail alone *(Croak!)*
> My never-ending chilling moan. *(Croak!)*
>
> I labor long,
> I have no rest— *(Croak!)*
> A banshee with a royal crest. *(Croak! Croak!)*

A banshee! Just your bad luck. You prepare yourself for some scary shrieking. But you have come this far, and you decide to enter the attic.

You think of your spells. You hate to use the important transformation spell this early in your adventure. You're not sure a shrunken banshee is any less dangerous than a full-size one, so you don't want to shrink it. And you don't think banshees have feet, so the inverse ointment won't work. That leaves you with Lunay's slumber dart and the mirror amulet.

If you want to offer this sleepless banshee a cure for its insomnia, withdraw the dart from your pouch and turn to page 51.

If you think the banshee will freeze with fear when it sees you as another banshee, hang the amulet around your neck and turn to page 101.

from page 65

You don't like the look of the pool of water, and remember that the attic was as dry as dust. You run to the linen closet and grab an armful of bedsheets. Then you bolt up the stairs to the attic, two steps at a time. *Slurp. Slurp.* The water has reached the corridor below.

Just before you enter the attic, you hear the banshee prince—now wide awake—shriek and wail, "EEEeeeyiiiheee! Guaardian, I'll eeeeat your head! My toooads! My dusssst!"

"Pirate," you whisper on the stairway, "I'm about to become a ghost. Take two bites out of this sheet, for eye holes, and then stand on my shoulder." You slip the sheet over your head, decorate it with a few strands of seaweed, and enter the attic.

"Guaarrdian!" The banshee screams in triumph at the sight of you. Moonlight washes over him from the hole in the ceiling. You wring your hands in mock despair under your sheet, and answer in a low, hollow voice.

"Oh, Great Prince, I am but the ghost of a guardian now, for I have been drowned in this miserable house."

"Eeeeeeiiiii!" The banshee laughs. "Now you shall guarrd eternallyyyy. This house siinks niiightly, drowning all withinnn. It riiises at dawnnn. But here in my aaattic, we all stay dryyy—as dryyy as dussst. Where is my dussst, Guardian?"

The banshee circles closer.

"It turned to mud in the water, sire," you answer sheepishly. You appear to be wringing your hands even harder now as under your sheet you knot together the linens you took from the closet.

"Great Prince," you say, "I know you are angry, and I will make up for the wrongs I have done. But I am still in shock at my sudden ghostly state. Please leave me alone with my thoughts for a short time."

The banshee considers this for a moment. "Yesss, it is difficult in the beginning. As you have helped meee find sleeep, I shall help yooouu. I shall perform a concert for yooouu. I shall call it 'Songs for a New Ghost.'" The banshee begins with an ear-piercing howl: "Ohhooooooo!" The toads join in.

You are relieved you are not really a ghost. You couldn't stand an eternity of such duets. The banshee has not left you alone, but it is busy singing, and you have finished making a rope of bedsheets. You center yourself under the hole in the ceiling and begin to sway back and forth, as though you are enjoying the concert. The banshee nods approvingly, closes his eyes, and howls even louder. "Ahooahooahooahooo!"

As you signal, the parrot flies out the hole and into the night, carrying one end of the rope in his beak. You hope he will be able to anchor it on the roof. The rope dangles just above your shoulders. Soon Pirate pokes his head back through the hole and winks. You jump onto the rope and pull yourself up to a standing position, your feet resting on the bottom knot. The banshee opens his eyes. "Oh, Prince," you cry. "From your music I am learning the true meaning of ghost-hood.

"See how I levitate! I rise into thin air! Please sing on!"

"My muuussic often has that efffect," answers the banshee. "Oooahoooahoooahooo!"

You begin to climb the rope. The knots hold. You are almost to the hole in the ceiling when the sheet you are wearing begins to slip off.

"EEeeeeiiiiyiiiii!" The banshee has discovered your trick. "You'll be a ghooost yet, Guaaarrdiann!" it shrieks.

You grip the rope and continue to shimmy up-ward. You feel an icy pain pass through one ankle, and suddenly the sheet pulls free. The banshee has missed your ankle and grabbed your disguise. The sheet falls slowly through the screaming banshee, who wrestles with its flapping corners. Your heart is racing and you are out of breath. You strain every muscle in your body to haul yourself onto the roof.

Pirate has wrapped the rope around an over-hanging tree limb. You climb onto the limb, loosen the rope, and cast it back through the hole in the roof, just as the banshee prince's howling mouth appears in the opening. His shrill cries are muffled as the rope passes through his misty banshee body and lands in a heap on the floor below.

You know the banshee won't leave his haunt—or his toads—so you are safe for now. Ignoring the shrieking, croaking, and slurping below, you concentrate on your surroundings. The rooftop is now an island in a murky lagoon. All around you are twisting trees. You search the darkness for swimming swamp creatures or night dwellers in the treetops. The moonlight reveals no dangers, and the silence is only broken by the ghostly racket from the Cottage of Caterwaul.

If you start to make your way through the treetops, turn to page 103.

If you would rather rest on the tree limb until daylight, turn to page 69.

from page 35

Hod's first army of mud men have had a day's head start marching toward Rilla. You are not sure you could catch up to them in time. You have a better chance to head off the clay soldiers marching on Fray. If the clay army attacks the Wizard of Fire, he will surely respond with fireballs, lightning bolts, and dragons' breath. And once the clay army is fired, the soldiers will be as hard and as strong as rock.

You marvel at the Earth Wizard's clever scheme to use the weapons of an enemy to his own advantage.

You watch the last of the marching mud men vanish into the forest night. The stream of light to the south disappears as the portal in Hod's mountainside silently closes.

Again you spy through the window of Hod's roof. The Wizard of Earth is heaving with laughter. He produces small cakes in the shapes of wizards' heads, one stuck on each finger. He pops a Rilla cake into his mouth with a cheerful "Yum!"

You sneak off to the south, on the trail of the clay army. The sluggish mud men are not hard to catch up with.

The clay soldiers are marching steadily but slowly. You notice that they are not very intelligent, and are easily confused. Often they bump into low-hanging branches or stumble on roots in their path.

Twice you observe fallen mud creatures, flat as pancakes, trampled by the rest.

You walk on, past soldier after soldier, until you reach the beginning of the line. The mud men are led by a crudely shaped officer, a clay figure like the others but somewhat larger. Decorative knobs protrude from his head, and he marches in advance of his charges, never looking back.

You could easily pass this awkward army and reach Fray's fortress before their attack, as you originally planned. But you also realize that you may be able to divert this clay army. If you wear your mirror amulet, the mud men will think you are one of them. You are tall enough to pass for their leader. Perhaps if you march in the front, they will follow you.

If you hurry ahead to warn Fray, turn to page 19.

If you want to try to take over Hod's clay army, turn to page 114.

from page 48

You decide to warn Rilla that Hod's clay army is on its way to attack her riverboat palace. You approach the wizardess on the shore.

"Hail, Wizardess of Water!" you say. Rilla turns gracefully away from her school of flying fish and regards you with serious eyes.

"A young apprentice!" she murmurs. "What can you want in this time of woe?"

"I come from my master Caladrius," you reply, "to invite you to a great Council of Wizards. But there is another matter, even more important to you right now. If you will hold back your attack on Syrrus, I can help you avoid a more urgent danger to your river world."

"What help can you be to me now?" Rilla demands sadly. "Syrrus must pay for his attack. I have summoned my army of fish. They cannot fly for long without water. But I will open a river all the way from here to Syrrus' Palace of Clouds. I will fill the path of Syrrus' cyclone with rushing water. It will tear through the forest, a fine wet road for my fish to follow. Begone, Apprentice!"

You retreat into the forest, but hide behind a tree to watch. Rilla begins to spin like a whirlpool. Droplets of water fly from her whipping hair in a circle of lights. You hear her chant.

*"Tidal wave, tidal wave,
A forest road of water pave.
Take the path Syrrus has flown
With the wrath of his cyclone!"*

Rilla raises her arms and calls to her fish.

Downstream a huge wall of water rises. A tidal wave! It stretches to the sky, then crashes to the shore. Its mighty weight drowns the forest floor and cuts down all in its way. It follows the already-flattened path of Syrrus' cyclone.

You scramble along the shoreline left in its wake. Then you climb to the top of a nearby hill. In the valley below you see hundreds of Hod's clay beings marching forward, ready to attack. They do not see the tidal wave bearing down on them until it is too late.

The mud men scatter in panic, but there is nowhere to run. The wave floods over the clay army with a terrible roar. Several of the mud soldiers grab trees, but they are swept up in the powerful wave and smashed down like helpless rag dolls.

As the clay army dissolves in the rushing water, the wave slows down and turns from green to brown. Soon the valley is a rich pool of mud. Rilla's tidal wave has dissolved Hod's clay army, but the melting army has stopped the tidal wave.

Then you begin to giggle. For Rilla's troop of flying fish have flocked into the valley behind the tidal wave and are now floundering in the mud. Those who work free of the goo fly back toward the riverboat, dripping brown muck on their friends stuck below.

You turn and see Rilla standing at your side.

"Yes, Apprentice," she says, nodding. "This foolishness has gone far enough. I will join this council of yours."

You hope that this will mean an end to the War of the Wizards.

THE END

98

You set off toward the fortress of Fray, the Wizard of Fire. Your pouch of spells hangs from your belt, and Pirate settles onto your shoulder for the ride.

You enter a clearing and sit down on a tree stump to examine your spells. *[There is a list of what you find on page 122. Please go to that page and then return.]*

You continue on your way, and walk for many miles. Toward late afternoon you notice that the moist earth beneath your feet has given way to dusty gray ash, and the air has grown hot. You hear thunder in the distance, and all other sounds have ceased. You see neither bird nor beast. The landscape, once green and fruitful, is now barren and charred.

Go to page 99.

At last you sight Fray's fortress. The sun is setting and the sky burns orange behind the dark structure. Seeing no guards, you venture closer.

The fortress looms before you, its sheer gray walls tapering to a tall cone. Flaming lava pours from the peak in festive streamers. The lava empties into a boiling moat but does not overflow. You wonder if it is recycled upward through the core of the fortress, an endless fountain of liquid fire.

You search for an entrance. All you find is one opening—a slit that widens, narrows, then disappears in shifting positions on the steep fortress wall.

The thunder has softened to a throaty rumbling, like the purr of a giant cat. You see no sign of Fray or his fireballs. To test for a lightning field, you toss a small stick toward the lava moat. You are rewarded with a sizzling flash, then a sprinkle of powder that was once the stick.

Wondering how to sneak into such a well-protected fortress, you consider your spells. With your transformation spell, you could turn yourself into a phoenix, the firebird, and find a way to fly inside. Or you could swim across the moat as a fire salamander, the flame quencher. But you wanted to save your transformation spell for an emergency. It is your most powerful spell—and you have no way to change yourself back.

Perhaps, if you wear the mirror amulet, Fray will think you are another Wizard of Fire. That would probably make him attack you, though.

You consider growing to a gigantic size and stomping out the fortress fire with your leather boot. But you are not sure the spell would make you large enough, and your mission is to bring Fray to the Council of Wizards, not to squash him.

Your other spells are of no help until you confront an enemy.

You don't think you can penetrate Fray's fortress unless you assume the form of a salamander or a phoenix, both immune to flames.

But there is a chance Fray will simply invite you in himself if you tell him you are a messenger from the other wizards, and you just want to talk.

If you call upon Fray to allow you to enter his fortress, turn to page 50.

If you decide to use your transformation spell, turn to page 16.

from page 87

The mirror amulet hangs heavily around your neck. You decide to test its effect on Pirate before you face the banshee, who is groaning loudly behind the attic door.

"Pirate, how do I look?" you whisper to the parrot.

Pirate looks you up and down with a critical eye.

"Parrot," he squawks in reply. "Handsome. Big improvement." He winks at you, and you wink back. The amulet is working.

You cautiously open the attic door and peer through the crack. You shiver with cold as a blast of freezing air rushes out. Then you shiver in fright as you see the banshee prince, a see-through form of blue-white mist, with teeth and nails like icicles and a hollow, frozen stare. "Ooohooohoooh," he moans as he inspects a line of dusty toads.

You slip into the attic and shut the door behind you. It is the dustiest place you have ever seen. Perhaps you will be able to hide in the swirling clouds of dust and the banshee won't notice you at all. You begin to sneak toward a trio of toads in a dark corner, but a dust ball is tickling your nose. *"Aah—aah—aah—chooooo!"* you roar.

"EEEeeeyiiiIII!" The banshee whirls to face you with a piercing shriek, but freezes in midair. A look of recognition steals over his haggard face. You remain still and silent for a moment until you remember that you are supposed to act like a banshee.

"Yiiieeeeee!" you scream in your highest voice, and you shake your hands in the air.

Suddenly the banshee rushes at you, his transparent arms outstretched. Before you can blink, you are trapped in his icy embrace.

"Grissselllda, my love," he moans and wails, "you have returned to meeee at laassst!" He hugs you tighter.

You had better start practicing your banshee shrieks. You may be living here for a long time to come.

THE END

You climb almost to the top of the tree. Pirate flies ahead to scout the area. You'd like to get far away from the Cottage of Caterwaul. You've got the toad dust you came for, and you're ready to resume your journey to Fray's fortress.

Massive trees encircle the spooky lagoon and stretch far into the swampland that borders Fray's domain. From the trees hang gray-green mosses and hairy brown vines.

You tug on the long vine nearest you. It is thick and sturdy, and will surely hold your weight. You spot an opening in a tree a short distance away, a barren branch within a cave of leaves. You tie the end of the vine around your waist, for safety's sake, and grip its firm stem an arm's length from your body. Then you take a deep breath and prepare to jump. You don't look at the weedy waters far below you.

You push off from your tree as hard as you can and swing away, across and up onto the open branch.

Your landing is rough—you land on your backside rather than your feet and have to hook your knees around the branch to keep your balance—but you are pleased. Swinging on vines is harder than it looks, but with practice it should get to be fun.

You look around for another vine. Your tree has no vines on it; it is a leafy tree with hanging moss.

Pirate will have to find the loose end of a vine in the next tree you choose and carry it to you in his beak.

"Pirate!" you call. The parrot lands on your shoulder with a squawk. You sight a dangling vine on the limb of a nearby tree.

"Pirate, please bring me that vine. We can fly through the treetops together." You begin to untie the first vine from your waist. Then you crouch on the branch and lean your back against the trunk of the tree, watching through a frame of leaves. Pirate gives you a cheerful wink, flies across to the curling vine, clamps his beak around it, and tugs sharply.

"Chachachachachacheeee!" You hear a grating shriek, and the leaves above the vine part, revealing a chattering swamp monkey. An astonished Pirate is biting the monkey's tail! The monkey's lips are curled far from his glinting teeth, and his eyes narrow in anger. With one powerful flick of his tail, he sends Pirate tumbling head over tail feathers.

The swamp monkey has caught sight of you. He is turning handsprings and gesturing wildly. He is twice your size, and a skilled acrobat. His fur is braided in warlike clumps, and his curving claws look sharp.

If you try to soothe him with an apology, turn to page 8.

If you reach for a spell, turn to page 117.

106

You are curious, and you hate to be impolite, but you have an important task ahead of you. You decide that you may need *all* your spells and that you have spent enough time with the dorkin trader.

"I mean no discourtesy," you tell him, "but I must decline your generous offer. I wish you a good journey. Perhaps we will meet again someday."

"It's your loss, Apprentice," answers the dorkin. "I'll just be on my way." He hurries down the path, the heavy sack over his shoulder, and is gone in the blink of an eye.

You hop to your feet in surprise. You didn't think he could move so fast. Wondering where he is off to, you decide to follow him.

Turn to page 32.

You look about the crystal maze. Even as you stand still, the walls of light and color shift and multiply around you. Surely one of your spells will help you to find your way out. You think about them one at a time.

You eliminate Lunay's slumber dart first. There is no one to put to sleep. Likewise, there is no one to look into your mirror amulet—and now it is invisible anyway. You think of the inverse ointment, which reverses all your movements. If you used it, you would be lost in reverse. You could use your transformation spell to change yourself into something else. But you would still be invisible and lost. You could shrink yourself, but then you would be tiny, invisible, and lost. Or you could grow and hope to burst out of the maze.

If you try your growing spell, turn to page 83.

If you change your mind and decide to explore further, turn to page 53.

108

from page 74

You don't want to offend the dorkin, and you are curious, so you agree to his trade. You hope there is a treasure in the dorkin's sack.

"Good, good, good!" The dorkin claps his hands and hops up and down. "A swap!"

"All right," you say. "First give me the sack."

"What manners you have," scolds the dorkin. "That is not how it's done. I have offered a trade, and you have agreed to it. Now *you* must give *me* the item you promised. We'll put the sack on the ground between us."

This arrangement seems safe enough to you. You will be able to claim the sack as soon as you give the dorkin a spell. Even if he tries to run away with the sack after he takes the spell, you know you can catch him—unless he *uses* the spell. You gulp. You hadn't thought of that. What if he shrinks you, or puts you to sleep, or turns you into a bug? You are suddenly very nervous. But you have made a promise, and it is too late to change your mind.

"Come, come," says the impatient dorkin. You take a deep breath and reach into your pouch. Your fingers close around a cool, metal box. You pull it out and hand it to the dorkin. It is the tin of inverse ointment, which reverses all your movements. You let out your breath in relief. It seems that you may have made a good trade after all. Won't Caladrius be proud if you return to the Castle of Changes a wealthy hero!

The dorkin examines the tin and crows with delight. "What's this? Wizard magic?" he asks. You realize that he can't read the label.

"It's for your feet," you reply. You are already busy untying the cord around the sack.

"Ah, my poor, tired feet," says the dorkin. He seats himself on a rock several yards away and begins to rub the ointment on his leathery feet.

You anxiously open the sack and peer inside. At the top you find a mass of leafy greens covering whatever is beneath. You grasp a handful of the tough leaves and pull. They don't budge! They must be attached to whatever they are hiding. You push the sack down to the ground in a wrinkled heap and stare in dismay. Your treasure is a giant turnip.

"There, you see!" says the dorkin triumphantly. "Trading brings treasure. That is a *prize* turnip. Dorkins love turnips."

You don't answer.

"I grew it myself!" he adds proudly.

You are angry, and feel you have been tricked. "Swap me back," you demand. "I want my ointment!"

"What's done is done," answers the dorkin. His feelings are hurt, and he takes several steps away from you, only to find himself closer to you than he was before. The inverse ointment is working. All of his movements are reversed. The dorkin looks confused.

"It's not fair!" you shout. "What do I want with a giant turnip? I *hate* turnips!"

You have frightened the dorkin, and he turns to run away, but he runs straight into you instead. You tumble over the huge turnip and land flat on the ground, on your stomach.

"You tricked me, you wicked dorkin," you cry, as you start to get up.

The dorkin tries to run away again, but he stomps over you instead. A smile flickers across his face as he begins to understand.

"Wicked, eh? Tricky, am I? You ungrateful apprentice, insulting my prize turnip!"

"I'm sorry!" you cry. "It's a wonderful turnip. Please forgive me." The dorkin extends his palm for a forgiving handshake. He tries to walk toward you and is soon gone. You are on your own—with a giant turnip.

THE END

You gather the loose bits of bird's nest around you and curl up for the night. You are tired and snug, and soon you are fast asleep.

At dawn you are abruptly awakened by a loud squawking above your head. You look up in horror. A roc, a giant bird, is swooping toward you, her ferocious claws bared, her shining blue wings flapping in distress. You are in her nest. Before you can react, the bird hauls you into the air, high above the treetops. The forest below looks like a bed of moss. Your mind is racing. You wonder if she will eat you or drop you. She seems to be flying almost straight up, higher and higher.

As you pass through the clouds, they gather into the shapes of towers and turrets, orchards, a stable, a gatehouse. It must be Syrrus' Palace of Clouds!

On and up you fly, past a cloudy drawbridge, over a misty moat, to the top of the highest tower. Set into its turret amid wisps of mist is another nest. It contains three baby rocs, each as large as you. You are rudely deposited in the nest. You squeeze your eyes shut and wait to be eaten by the ravenous rocs. When nothing happens, you venture a peek at your nestmates. They have small, bony heads, curious eyes, and bluish feathers across their necks and backs. You realize with dismay that except for their beaks and

claws, they look just like your bald and befeathered self. The great mother roc must have mistaken you for a fallen rocling!

The mother bird is flying away. You must try to explain to her—perhaps she will carry you back home. But she is already out of sight.

You peer over the edge of the nest. It is a sheer drop to the base of the tower. You'd better stick with your new brothers and sisters, and hope that Caladrius spots you soon in his crystal ball.

THE END

114

You decide to lead Hod's army away. Fray need never know an attack was planned. You slip the mirror amulet over your head and fall into place, in between the clay officer and the first soldier in line. None of the creatures notices a difference. The amulet must be working!

You begin to slow your steps, little by little, as the officer marches farther ahead of you. Soon he veers off to the right, and you veer to the left. You glance over your shoulder and see Hod's clay army trooping behind you. One after another the mud men follow you through the woods. You feel like a snake's head: your body is so long you cannot see your tail. All you know is that it is coiling somewhere behind you.

Now that your plan has succeeded, you wonder what you should do with your new army. You have never had such power before. You could attack Fray yourself! But a fight is what you have been trying to prevent. You could bring them to Caladrius. But what would he want with an army of mud men? You could march the soldiers back to Hod and attack his mound. That would teach him a lesson!

You lead your troops in a long, slow curve, back the way you came. Soon you are climbing Hod's mossy mountain once again. From within, the wizard's snores reach your ears. You circle the mound, but no door is visible. Up you march to the roof. How will you be able to get inside?

You stop marching when you reach the roof window, and you bend down to look through it. You can see Hod lying below you, fast asleep amid half-eaten cakes and jugs of cider. His snores vibrate the earth.

You are about to straighten up and halt your troops when something from behind bumps into you and sends you sprawling. You somersault to your feet in surprise. When you turn, you see that the first clay soldier has fallen across the window and the second has tripped over the first. Now the third and fourth soldiers pile onto the first two. Will the glass give way?

"Halt! Halt!" you command, raising your palms in the air. But still the rude beings advance and pitch forward.

With a cracking sound the window breaks, and the mound of mud men collapses through the hole. *Crash!* The snoring stops with a sputter, and Hod roars with anger.

"What are you doing, fools? To Fray! Fray!" But he is unable to get up. One after another the mud creatures fall through the hole and flatten on his well-filled belly. Hod continues to shout at the raining mud men, but he is soon buried in a huge heap of soft clay. Still more creatures pour through the hole to their doom.

You hear Hod's muffled cries and decide that you'd better make sure he is all right. You slide down the mountain of clay, now piled almost to the roof, and dig Hod's head out from the bottom.

"I thank you," says Hod with relief. "Who are you? Another Wizard of Earth?" You remember that you are still wearing your mirror amulet. You remove it from your neck.

"I am Simon, apprentice to Caladrius," you say, "and I beg you to make peace with Rilla and Fray and all other wizards. You see how your own power has worked against you."

"I do indeed." Hod sighs, looking at his monumental mound of mud. "I never really wanted to be Supreme Wizard, you know. I just want to garden and to bake cakes with the help of my clay companions."

"If you will call back the attack on Rilla, and the lone officer marching on Fray, I will gladly dig you out," you say. "Then you must accompany me to the Castle of Changes, to attend the Council of Wizards."

"I give you my word," Hod replies.

You and Hod are soon in sight of the Castle of Changes. The flag of the council is flying, and you are proud of the part you have played in ending the War of the Wizards.

THE END

from page 104

The swamp monkey is screeching and waving his arms. Will he attack? He beckons to you as if daring you to fight. You decide to shrink him, but you won't be able to reach him from your tree. You'll have to enlist Pirate again, to spill the potion on the monkey. You pull the little bottle from your pouch. The parrot shudders, shakes his head, and ruffles his feathers.

"R-r-ready." He winks. You uncork the bottle, and Pirate takes it in his beak.

The swamp monkey points a claw at you and continues his scolding chatter. He reaches for a vine.

"Now, Pirate!" you order. The parrot bursts through a cluster of leaves, flutters above the screaming monkey, and empties the bottle over its head.

The ferocious monkey shrinks! His voice changes to a speedy squeak. He gets smaller and smaller, but he doesn't run away. Even when his shrinking slows and he is only one foot high, he continues to jump up and down, point at you, and squeak.

In a flurry of feathers, Pirate settles next to the monkey, now his own size, and squawks at you proudly. Then he, too, begins to jump and squawk, huge-eyed with fear. "R-r-run!" he squawks, and he tosses you a vine.

That's when you look behind you into the gaping jaws of a giant snake.

THE END

118

from page 68

You decide that a roomful of wizards can surely take care of themselves, so you think of a plan of your own.

You take Lunay's animal friends to the armory. There you find helmets and breastplates for yourself, the bear, the raven, and the nighthawk, and a full suit of armor for the stallion. Then you search for suitable weapons. You find battle axes, lances, spears, and bows, but none seems quite right.

The two creatures you have never seen before are making odd noises and sniffing at a cabinet against a wall. You open the cabinet and find a stack of slender black tubes, all labeled in a spidery hand. They are night darts—created by Lunay! You search for a spell you can use against Fray. *Dream dart, love dart, star dart, slumber dart*. You choose the slumber dart.

You throw a black cloak around your shoulders and proceed to a battlement high above the courtyard. There you make your battle plans with the animals. The night is black, and there is no sign of Caladrius or the others.

Suddenly the night sky is split by a jagged lightning bolt. It pierces a window below you with a splintering crash. You know it was the window next to the Council Chamber. Fray has made his entrance.

Not wanting to waste any time, you mount Lunay's winged stallion. The sable climbs up behind you, and together you soar into the air, camouflaged in darkness.

You can see Fray, lit against the dark sky, as he snaps his fingers to light a spiraling fireball. The stallion glides behind Fray as the fireball bursts into flame. You are glad Fray does not see you yet.

"Hiding, are you?" he bellows, as he hurls the blazing comet at the castle. "Come out, wizards, and fight."

You signal the attack.

Fray snaps his fingers and a small flame appears. He is about to create another fireball when the flame goes out with a *poof!* Fray grumbles and snaps his fingers again. This flame too is blown out. The raven and the nighthawk are doing their jobs well, beating out the flames with their powerful wings.

You grip the slumber dart, and the stallion swoops close to Fray. You aim for one of Fray's bare arms. The rest of him is protected. But now the Fire Wizard sees you. He pitches a lightning bolt at your head. The stallion leaps over it, as if jumping a fence, and charges directly at Fray. The Fire Wizard roars and grabs for another lightning bolt.

As Fray pulls back his arm to aim, the sable jumps from behind you and lands on Fray's face. He clings to the wizard from ear to ear, a dark fur blindfold, and Fray loses his balance and drops the lightning bolt.

The stallion dives close again, and you send the dart flying into Fray's shoulder, right on target.

With one more great swoop the stallion catches the tumbling body of slumbering Fray. You land gracefully in the courtyard and deposit the sleeping wizard on the stone floor. The bear sits on him, just to make sure he can't escape, and the wolf and the panther guard his head and feet.

"Wonderful, Simon!" you hear Caladrius say.

"A marvelous plan," Rilla says with a laugh.

"Perhaps you should be a Wizard of Animals," says Lunay with admiration.

"Where were you?" you demand. "You left me to do everything myself!"

"And you did splendidly," answers Caladrius. "Congratulations! You have passed a wizard's first test—for courage and inventiveness in time of danger. You'll be a great wizard soon enough. For the next years of your training you will have the privilege to study with each one of us in turn. Then you may choose a specialty and venture out on your own."

"You can have my job as Fire Wizard," Fray says, groaning and rubbing his eyes. "I give up. Please ask this bear to move!"

Laughing and joking, you and the wizards follow the smell of a grand banquet. You troop into the castle to celebrate your success.

THE END

You open the leather pouch.

First, you withdraw Lunay's slumber dart. Burned into the cork blocking one end of the tube is the word "blow." The opposite cork reads "dart."

Next you find a small vial of a sparkling dust marked "One Transformation—Rhyme Not Included." You are pleased. This spell will allow you to change something into something else.

You dig into the pouch again and pull out a bottle of inky liquid and a tin of waxy ointment. The tin is labeled "Inverse Ointment—*Apply to feet for backward movement.*" The bottle is labeled

> Sprinkle me on friend or foe;
> I will make him shrink or grow.
> If you want him to diminish,
> Spill me out until I finish.
> If you want him to expand,
> Throw me twice from your right hand.

At the bottom of the pouch, you find an amulet on a chain. It is an oval piece of metal with a diamond-shaped sliver of mirror set in its center. On the back are engraved the words "He who looks at me sees another like himself."

You are not sure exactly what all the spells will do, but you feel safer knowing you have them.

You make a mental list of the spells you have found: 1 Slumber Dart, 1 Transformation, 1 Backward Movement spell, 1 Shrink or Grow spell, 1 mirror amulet. Total number of spells: 5.

Please go back to the page from which you came.